parts of speech

ISBN: 978-1-961753-00-6 (Paperback)
ISBN: 978-1-961753-01-3 (Ebook)

LCCN: 2023910986

First Edition

10 9 8 7 6 5 4 3 2

Black and Square
Hampton Roads, VA

Tender and strange, startling and lyrical, witty and nuanced, Ran Walker's stories lingered in my mind long after I finished reading them.

Grant Faulkner, Executive Director of NaNoWriMo and Co-Founder of 100 Word Story

I'm amazed that Ran Walker can stuff so much meaning and power into so few words.

Rion Amilcar Scott, award-winning author of Insurrections and The World Doesn't Require You

parts of speech

100-Word Stories

Ran Walker

Viewed freely, the English language is the accretion and growth of every dialect, race, and range of time, and is both the free and compacted composition of all.

Walt Whitman

contents

part three
blackness

part four
writers

part one
hypnagogia

somniloquy

S OMETIMES HE TALKED in his sleep, much of it aggressive, angry threats aimed at someone who was not there—at least she hoped not. She thought about waking him to tell him what he'd been doing, but she didn't feel safe enough to do that. Instead, she would recount the previous night's episode to him over breakfast, where he'd laugh and tell her he had no idea what she was talking about. She asked if he might want to see someone about this, but again she was met with laughter. It frightened her, though, that he hated someone that much.

gum

HE STOOD BY, idly watching his friend open the mega-pack of chewing gum she'd bought from the bodega. As she unwrapped the first piece, he thought she might offer him a stick. To his surprise, though, she continued unwrapping and stuffing each of the pieces of gum into her mouth—now realizing her mouth was much larger than it initially appeared—and he watched her cheeks as she chewed the entire pack of gum at once, her eyes staring off into the distance, as if he were not there and that an enormous chewing gum bubble would carry her away.

freeze

SHE WAS ALWAYS TOLD that her father was killed by officers because he refused to freeze when they told him to. So, as she stood on the abandoned football field, still frozen from a game of Freeze Tag hours earlier (the other kids had left for dinner), she dared not move. Even when she saw the black sedan circling the block several times. The sedan stopped beside the field, and a masked grown-up emerged. If that person touched her, she would be unfrozen. Then she could run home. By that time, though, she now understood it would be too late.

dreams

6

She whispers into his ear, telling him about a dream—a fantasy—she had about him the previous night. He willingly listens—has no place he'd rather be than on the receiving end of this story—his ear canal tickled by not just her warm breath, but the ideas she shares. Soon it will be his turn to return the favor, to share his dream about her. The problem is that he has never dreamed about her, though he still longs to be with her. He dreams of falling from the sky, but his story will leave out this part.

existential

He never really felt his age.

When he was younger, he felt older. When he was older, he felt younger.

That he never felt completely in sync with his body remained one of the great mysteries of his life. His peers seemed to be at ease with the trajectories of their lives. They had accepted that life was a particular thing and began their slow walk toward their graves.

He often questioned the purpose of life—until he realized such things were futile. He'd live in each moment until there were no more, and maybe—just maybe—he'd find peace.

moment

SHE STARES at her mother's body, trying to hold on to every single detail of this moment. Pictures aren't the same. All they do is create a barrier between you and the experience, and she doesn't want that.

She needs to remember the peace on her mother's face one last time. This moment, she hopes, will erase the memories of those last months of pain and sickness.

The crematorium will erase from existence all that lies before her, leaving her with whatever memory survives this moment.

She closes her eyes, clinging to every bit of her mother she'll ever have.

cube

ONE MORNING he awoke inside of a windowless, doorless cube. Seeing no exit, he began trying to calculate how much breathable air he had left. Having awakened there, he had no idea of how long he'd been inside the cube or how much air he'd already used up. Unable to suppress his panic, he knocked on each of the walls and screamed out —all to no avail. Realizing he was alone, with limited air left, he sat in the corner of the cube, taking shallow breaths. He finally decided to sleep, hoping he'd eventually awaken to a very different reality.

bass

Few knew her secret.

She'd spent years cultivating a particular image, one her fans loved. Directors, producers, actors, and craft services were equally unaware. She'd managed to perfect her voice, hiding evidence of its deep resonance, warming it up hours ahead of interactions, twisting it upward to make it bright, to fit the character she portrayed to the rest of the world.

She often wondered what would come of her career if the world discovered how deep her voice really was—that she was a bass and not an alto—but dispelled the notion.

Some things were better left unsaid.

afrosurrealism

IN HIS DREAM, he is having brunch with a young writer who was slain by a transit cop in the weeks that followed another 1968 assassination. On the other side of the table sits a young multi-hyphenate artist who just completed work on a critically-acclaimed television series that ran for four seasons. He is asking these men how to traverse the surrealism of being a Black man in America. One from Arkansas, the other from Georgia, they smile. They know I am from Mississippi, so, by default, I must already possess the answer to my question. And they are right.

headlock

The world-famous Afroed astrophysicist has the alien in a headlock. I can barely hear the conversation, but it seems like there is a question that the astrophysicist demands the alien answer, and the alien doesn't appear to be particularly forthcoming. Maybe it is some fundamental truth about the universe that has, up until this moment, eluded all of humankind—and if this alien has its way, it will continue to elude us. But the astrophysicist is determined. He has in his arsenal several wrestling moves and mind-bending equations sure to stump our visitor. I watch in anticipation, with bated breath.

signs

He understood well why there was a "Stop" sign. It was exceedingly clear that a yield sign wouldn't work in many situations. There were too many scenarios where merely slowing down and checking for traffic wouldn't suffice. For example, if you were at a busy intersection, it would be impossible to know how to safely proceed without some kind of instruction. What if there was a pedestrian pulling a shopping cart or a mother pushing a stroller? "Stop" made plenty of sense, thus the need for the sign. What he couldn't understand, however, was why there wasn't a "Go" sign.

automatism

SHE DREAMED HIM, then drew him, then found him, then loved him, then threw him away and began again. This continued five more times, before her lover responded, "I have dreamed you, too, and I know you will want to let me go, as you did the others, but I cannot allow that. I hope you understand this." This terrified her, this threat, this attempt to disrupt the natural order of things, so she waited until he went to sleep and fell asleep beside him. In her dream she decided to kill him, and when she awoke, he was gone.

paralysis

IT TOOK him weeks to concoct the best position for sleeping. At first he tried his side, but he quickly found out that the arm he lay on would become nearly numb from his body's weight. Then he tried an odd, slanted splay, which he found too difficult to maintain. Ultimately, he decided to sleep on his stomach, one hand resting by his hip, the other near his head. It would have to work because he knew sleeping on his back was no longer an option. He didn't dare tempt the witch to return to sit on his chest again.

shadows

No one paid mind to the children holding hands and dancing in a circle, their voices singing in unison about monsters emerging from the dark woods and returning to eat all of the adults, each line of their rhyming stanzas as light as feathers tickling the soles of babies' feet, the sounds so soothing and innocuous that the adults ignored their conjurings, and it was only when the grizzly shadows emerged, enveloping the village, that they realized their children had orchestrated their demise and that their children's playful melodies would ultimately haunt them in the last moments of their lives.

ugly

His book was ugly. Beautifully, poetically ugly. "Banned by over 500 school districts" ugly. "Discussed in the same breath as Morrison, Nabokov, and Salinger" ugly. "Monique's character in *Precious*" ugly. "Children falling asleep hungry" ugly. "Hypocritical preacher" ugly. "Ugly cry when you lose a loved one" ugly. "Furnace in July" ugly. "Christmas sweater" ugly. "Bullies teaming up to beat down an innocent kid" ugly. "Parents fighting in front of their kids" ugly. Nightmare ugly. Unforgivably ugly. Downright fucking ugly. Uglier than the sound of the word in the mouth of evil.

But it wasn't uglier than the racism it portrayed.

poltergeist

He walked the corridor of the mansion, oblivious to the warnings he'd received earlier in the day. There was a malevolent force that lingered in certain spaces, in particular a room at the end of the hall on the third floor. Always a pragmatist, he felt too much was made of haunted spaces. People heard what they wanted to hear and saw what they wanted to see, manifesting things from their imaginations. So, when he found himself casually strolling the third floor that evening, he was shocked when he felt the deathly pull of something that refused to let him go.

carnival

THE BAND, in colorful masks and top hats, plays a drunken carnival song, as the demented clowns dance around in circles, half skipping to the minor melody, the crowd members now afraid to look away for even a second for fear they might turn back and see the face of evil inches from their faces. A carnival barker yells, "Step right up!" A geek grins, the blood of a headless chicken dripping down his chin. And the clowns dance and dance, while the band plays, the trumpets blaring their nightmarish cacophony and a lone saxophone bends itself into a pretzel.

necrophilia

HE PLAYED a zombie on a hit TV show, but his partner preferred he come home in costume and role play with her, where she would pretend to be afraid of him, before tearing away his already torn clothes and kissing his bare skin beneath the makeup. At first, he rather enjoyed the idea of doing something different, but as the season progressed and her kisses moved to the latex, he began to feel uncomfortable. Finally, he started having the makeup removed before he returned home, much to his partner's chagrin. Shortly afterwards, they parted ways for reasons never discussed.

sweven

SHE DREAMED of her boyfriend from high school every night as she lay next to her husband. She could feel his quiet kisses tickling her neck and feel his fingers studying the curves of her taut body. When she awoke next to her husband, his arm resting lazily on her round body, she felt safe and loved, but guilty all the same. It were as if her mind existed in two different bodies, one trapped in time, the other continuing to age.

"You're beautiful," her husband said, apropos of nothing.

She smiled, trying to ignore the dreams that awaited her.

chocoholic

She oftentimes complimented him on his complexion, comparing him to milk chocolate. Occasionally, he found her exoticizing his skin kind of sexy, the way she would press her skin against his and remark at the contrast by saying, "We're a swirl," but other times, he found it tiring and disconcerting. She was a chocoholic, she would remind him, and he was her life-size candy bar.

Then one morning he awoke to her licking the length of his body, savoring the taste of him. He enjoyed it so much, he barely noticed that she'd begun to sink her teeth into him.

part two
timing

arrhythmia

It would happen in the quietest of moments, when all seemed to be perfect around him, the deep pause of his heart, for a moment feeling like he was being pulled downward before the beat would return and he'd pass it off as gas or any number of things that could produce that uneven effect in his chest. He wondered if one day he might have a pause where the beat never returned, and the feeling frightened him, each pause a possible foreshadowing for the inevitable.

Rather than fear what he couldn't control, he decided, instead, to cherish every beat.

arms

26

IT WAS the warmth of his shoulders and his back when she held him that made her fall for him. His smile wasn't much to write home about, and if she were to be completely honest with herself, he wasn't particularly attractive. He wasn't smooth with his words. Even his laugh was corny.

Still, she couldn't explain it—this feeling, the feeling like he could shield all of the bad things in the world from her, that this unlikely person could provide a space that felt so safe that she could lie down in his arms and rest there forever.

kisses

She had her doubts.

He kissed her with his eyes open, something she noticed only after opening hers to see if his were closed.

"Do you always kiss me with your eyes open?" she'd asked.

"Yes."

"Why?"

"I don't know. That's the way I've always kissed."

It should have been a small, dismissible thing, but if he'd always done this—and he was single—maybe this was a sign

But she kissed with her eyes closed all the time—and she was single, too—so maybe she was over-thinking things.

Still, something in her sensed their days together were numbered.

jazz

THERE WAS a time when his fingers moved like lightning, kissing the ivory in elaborate glissandos, his dexterity plucking chromatic intricacies from the ether. But arthritis now shackled his hands, locking them in chains that made it challenging to play even a scale. Still, his mind danced with possibilities, improvisations to the chord progressions he read from old lead sheets. Occasionally, he made appearances, accepting roses for his contributions to the canon, but the tributes were always more acid than salve, as he longed to be among those playing, living in the glory of his youth until his last breath.

breaths

29

WHEN SHE WAS A CHILD, she would lay her head upon her father's chest and listen to his heart beat, her head rising and falling as he inhaled and exhaled. When she was in high school, she felt she was too old to do such a thing, but on difficult days, she found comfort in returning to her childhood habit. After her divorce, she found herself sobbing onto his chest, seeking solace in those deep breaths. Now, as he lay in hospice care, she carefully lay her head upon his fragile chest, feeling those breaths that anchored her slip away.

song

Miss Anne liked to sing the same song every Sunday. It wasn't in our hymnals, and our pianist learned it only by listening, but she sang it to the point we all knew it. Shortly after Pastor Robinson closed his sermon, you could hear Miss Anne's hum crescendoing from the back of the sanctuary, where she ushered. People would use her voice like a lantern, finding their way to the mourner's bench. And we sang along, her words imprinted on our hearts like memorized prayers. When she went home to glory, we kept right on singing her song each Sunday.

friends

When he was single, she was in a relationship. When she was single, he was in a relationship. Both knew that the relationship of their lives existed with the other, but neither could get the timing right. After a while, the hope they held began to wither, as doubts slowly crept into their minds, telling them that they would be better off as friends, that they had too much to lose by taking that step. So, when they were finally both single, they decided not to pursue the other, which turned out to be the biggest mistake of their lives.

mispronunciations

SHE FANCIED HERSELF A FASHION AFICIONADO, though she often wrestled with the pronunciation of colors. "Mauve" and "taupe" had an "aw" sound instead of the proper long "o," "Baroque" sounded like the former president's first name, and "cobalt" may as well have been a desert made of pastry and fruit. Still, she mispronounced these names with the kind of authority reserved for a person who felt just because she said it that it was correct. Those who enjoyed her video content refused to correct her, as her mispronouncing the colors incorrectly was yet another part of the entertainment they enjoyed.

time

When I was growing up, it was all about the Baby Boomers. Now, I see videos on Instagram seeking to explain the idiosyncrasies of Generation X, kids holding up my childhood toys with wonder, unable to fathom a world without the Internet or smartphones. They are befuddled by the fact I actually wore a key around my neck, tucked under my t-shirt to let myself into my house after school or that I watched a TV that had a knob and rested on top of another TV.

Even my childhood crushes are now senior citizens.

Where does the time go?

prom

The car fogged up so quickly they could hardly see beyond the windshield. Alone at last, they unbuckled their seatbelts and reclined their seats, eagerly reaching for each other in the darkness of country night. The clock display gave them two hours before her curfew, and the mixtape he'd made for the moment played softly beneath their thick kisses, as their fingers worked feverishly to undress the other. They clung to each other's slippery body, believing what they had would survive graduation. Only the blue lights of the police cruiser beaming through the windshield could bring them back to reality.

2064

SHE PLAYED THE KEYS, and he strummed his guitar, and while they created beautiful music, it was nothing like the magic they continually created in each other's life every single day: a soft kiss on the forehead here, a soft rub of the back there, kind words throughout the day, attentive intimacy, whispers of a life shared beyond the trials of their pasts, their melodies now intertwined in such a way the music they performed onstage now became a byproduct of the music they lived and breathed and shared offstage, her keys playing, his guitar strumming, their music continually growing.

video

IN THE END, he had to chalk it up to two things: bad judgment and underestimating his wife's strength. His plan was to put on the monster mask he'd bought from the Halloween store and crouch down beside the bed, then tap her until she woke. He expected her to scream and flail around, something entertaining for the video he'd planned to upload to his social media account, but when she came to, she didn't scream. Instead, she jumped up and kicked him so hard he fell into the bedroom wall, denting it.

That, too, made for an entertaining video.

soundtrack

It was the music that made her cry, much more than the movies themselves. She couldn't explain the reasoning, other than some chords and words, when combined, created an emotional elixir that transported her beyond the screen into the cobwebs of her own memories, a place where everyone in her world was different—younger—with much of the world still ahead of them. The songs reminded her of who she was before she settled into her adult life. It held her youth in its hands delicately like she imagined God would have done in that song she learned in kindergarten.

dancing

WHEN HIS PARENTS had their friends over to play Spades, inevitably they would interrupt him from doing his homework in the other room to come and provide mid-game entertainment.

His father would pop in the *Thriller* cassette and order him to do that "Michael Jackson shit" he enjoyed doing when he was alone in his room, doors closed, music turned down so low that more sound might come from a mouse pissing on cotton.

He wanted to protest—although he knew his father didn't play that—but when "Wanna Be Starting Somethin'" started up, his little body ultimately betrayed him.

titles

How DO you know when you are a novelist or a photographer or an artist or an emcee or a poet or a dancer or a filmmaker or a sculptor or an actor or even a microfictionist? Where does the line exist between being one who aspires and one who actually does? Is it measured in a certain number of hours that, on paper, seems beyond daunting? Is it determined by critics who've never attempted those arts themselves or the academics who've only written papers about them? Maybe it's just a matter of declaring something so that you believe it.

благодарность
Gratitude

THE EMCEE LOOKED out into the ocean of fans at the foot of the stage, many of them unable to speak any English beyond the lyrics of his songs. They rocked their heads in unison as the bass poured from the speakers, and for a moment, he thought back to his childhood days of making beats in his bedroom, battling and losing against kids at school who'd since given up on dreams of music. He thought about what he might've become had fate not dealt him this hand. He held the mic up to the crowd, tears filling his eyes.

blues

41

THEY TOOK the beast out of the jungle, its native habitat, and placed it in a zoo, behind thick steel bars, so that spectators could look at it, analyze it, study it, or ignore it. Most people only knew the beast from its presence in zoos and, therefore, found no reason to fear it or to imagine how powerful it may have been in the wild. It was safe and nonthreatening, and any kid with even an inkling of interest could easily walk up to the bars and place his fingers on its matted fur without any fear of repercussion.

mastication

SHE HATED the way he chewed his food. "Chew" seemed like too insignificant a word for it. "Masticate" seemed more appropriate. She hated the way he *masticated* his food. It was almost beast-like, the way his tongue and teeth worked together to grind his food for digestion. It felt almost *scientific*, how she viewed him, this mammal masticating its food. How had she allowed herself to be with a masticating mammal like this? Would they one day have children who would masticate their food, too, and she be in a house full of masticating mammals? She'd leave before that happened.

fan

One afternoon he ran into her at the grocery store. He recognized her immediately, her small stature standing next to an arrangement of tropical fruit piled higher than her height. He was indeed a fan, had even seen her perform on her bass in five different cities. He had once bought front-row seats to see her perform, where he and his date for that evening stood, side by side, fingers interlocked, swaying to music for two hours straight. Now, she was there. He started to go over and speak to her, but, at the last moment, decided not to intrude.

pronunciations

44

He was the kind of person who, once a person had established the pronunciation of a word for the conversation (for example "advertisement" with a long "I"), would deliberately make things awkward by going with a less preferred (yet still technically accurate) pronunciation, just to be different. He seemed to relish in these uneven, uneasy conversations, as if he were prepared to die upon this small hill just to prove a point, one that only caused him to appear unnecessarily contrary and small. Those inclined to converse with him preferred to let him talk first, hoping to return the favor.

part three
blackness

lie

HE STANDS in front of his class, likely the first Black professor they have ever had, and he looks past the rolling of eyes and beyond the oppugning of his words, holding on to his pedagogical skills like a lifebuoy. He'd never been this acutely aware of the scrutiny he received from his white students, their disdainful questioning of whether he was indeed bright enough to teach them. Had it always been like this and there was just limited license to show it, or had this been brought on by a white congressman challenging a Black president with one word?

beef

He took his cues from hip hop: beef helps to sell more records—well, books in this case. But he wasn't the kind of writer to go and pick a fight with other writers. At a fundamental level, he understood the challenges of creating any kind of art, whether good or bad, and could not bring himself to go *in* on other writers for simply doing their best.

So he created a pseudonym, one he could spar with. He'd draft both of their works, and hopefully his theories about beef would work to help him sell more books for them both.

conjuring

GRANDMA DIDN'T BELIEVE in witchcraft, but she was known for conjuring an amazing sweet potato pie. Occasionally, she'd use those sweet potatoes to make candied yams—which were technically not yams, but they were good all the same.

Granddad didn't believe in anything, but he could ferment any relative of a grape he could grow in the loam of his backyard. He'd make wine from scuppernongs and muscadines mainly, sweet liquor that would make a vintner cringe, but it was good all the same.

I haven't figured out what I believe yet, but I know I'll conjure something one day.

sneakergram

In an effort to create a different kind of sneaker Instagram account, he decided to take pictures of his sneakers as he sat on the toilet, his pants bunched just above the tops of his shoes. At first he did it to be ironic and humorous, but then his posts began to go viral. Suddenly, sneaker companies starting sending him shoes to debut on his porcelain throne, and even toilet paper companies wanted in on the action. Soon other influencers began posting similar photos, and it became a "thing." He tried creating other trends, but none was ever as successful.

bacon

HER NAME WAS BAYONCA, and she smelled like bacon. Maybe it was the cooked lye in her hair, the byproduct of Big Mama's hot comb pulling at her thick hair to reveal a beautiful brown, oiled scalp. Junior didn't know—didn't really care. He just knew that there was something to be said about a woman who smelled like a hearty breakfast, something that made him feel relaxed—dare he admit, comforted?—by it all. The other boys in class liked Erica, who smelled like flowers and candy, and that was cool, because he wanted to Bayonca all to himself.

tidsoptimist

52

THE MODEL ARRIVED LATE to his meeting with the reference book company, but in need of money, he booked the gig, sight unseen, to pose for a photo that would accompany one of the selected vocabulary words.

"Tidsoptimist?" he said. "What kind of made-up word is that?"

"It means to be habitually late," the representative informed him.

"Oh," he responded. "Is this because I'm Black and you think all Black people are late? That's so racist!"

The representative politely reminded him that he'd been the one to approach them about this particular job—after having arrived late for their meeting.

sticker

THE BARACK OBAMA 2008 sticker was faded and nearly peeling off the bumper of his sedan, but he refused to remove it. There was barely enough ink there to read, but he knew what had been there—what it had represented to him and millions of others—and it gave him a comforting feeling, reminding him there was actually a point in recent memory where a Black man had served two terms in the highest office in the land.

After 2020, it had become increasingly more challenging to remember those days, but the bumper sticker was there to remind him.

kids

54

THE PRANK WAS TOO ELABORATE, the frogs and all. The old man probably hadn't read *Exodus* in decades, if ever, so pouring the amphibians from the roof of his house was a fool's errand, not to mention trespassing. When the old man noticed the frogs on his lawn, he groaned, as if to say, "Again?" The thing is that we were unaware of any other time someone might have done this prank on him. Was he old enough to have been a Biblical Egyptian? We didn't really know. Nonetheless, we had failed in our prank, it being elaborate and all.

elsewhere

ALTHOUGH I HAD LEFT my hometown years earlier, I was not surprised to read about it in a major national newspaper. The incident involved one of my classmate's daughters having to share her valedictorian status with a white student who had taken easier, non-honors classes to boost his GPA. This incident reminded me of how, thirty years earlier, we'd had two homecoming queens—and two of nearly everything else. The biggest difference now, though, was that I was no longer living there, personally experiencing these shenanigans. Instead, I was having to read about this nonsense from elsewhere in the world.

boston

MY GRANDFATHER TAUGHT me to play Spades when I was six. It became our way of communicating. The rules were straightforward: no Jokers, no throwing in hands, no extra trumps. Each game taught me to be smart, to not do things without purpose, to not be afraid to rely on others for help.

Before he transitioned, he and I played as partners against my uncle and my friend. We ran our first and only Boston as a team. It was fated to be the last time I would play with him, but I would never forget what he taught me.

uninterested

SHE DIDN'T WASTE any time turning down his invitation to the prom. She tried to soften the blow by saying she simply wasn't interested, but later that week, her friends began to spread word that she thought he was corny and dressed funny.

Rumors, evolving as they often do, gradually made reference to his personal hygiene and his haircut (a poorly blended fade).

Years later, at their 20th class reunion, seeing how wealthy and handsome he'd become, she apologized to him for the "misunderstanding" years earlier, offering to buy him a drink.

He listened, but she knew he wasn't interested.

hair

MINDLESSLY SCROLLING through his social media feed one evening, he came across a random video of a young woman washing and combing nearly two feet of pubic hair from beneath a pair of athletic shorts. She washed the hair as one might wash the hair on their head, detangling, combing, and rinsing. It was the kind of image that took more than a few moments to realize what was going on. Once she dried it, she proceed to do an odd kind of braiding where she then carefully tucked it away. *The cost of going viral has risen*, he reasoned.

grilling

My uncle loved grilling but had no idea of how to do it properly. Determined to have the biggest fire ever, he would pour far too much lighter fluid on the coals. He also never cleaned his grill, insisting the burned crud on the grill frame was extra "seasoning" for the meat. He also overcooked everything that touched the grill, leaving the meat so dry that my little cousins would pour tap water over it. Still, no one could get him off the grill. We knew to just let him do his thing, sit back, and hope for the best.

retired

After having worked at a corporate job for fifteen years, and having served as a hall of fame ass kisser, he was now officially done with the respectability politics. No more navy blue suits and red ties. No more cap-toed Oxfords and starched white shirts. No more haircuts that helped to make him more identifiable to white executives. He was done with it all. From here forward, he would be growing his hair out, wearing jeans, rocking kicks, and sporting t-shirts and hoodies. He would disappear into his Blackness, and his employers would never see or hear from him again.

fop

EVEN AS A CHILD, he wore bowties to school. He would meticulously tie them in the mirror before putting on his blazer and loafers. The kids in his class had a field day making jokes about him. Even his teachers would occasionally ask him if he was available to do their taxes in the spring. He took it all in stride, though, determined to wear his bespoke clothing, paid for by odd jobs. He may not have been the best student, but he was by far the best dressed—at least in his mind—and that surely accounted for something

grammarian

CONVERSATE. Comfortability. Irregardless.

The debates about Oxford commas.

Split infinitives.

And the endless problem with modifiers.

His love of grammar had complicated his personal life in too many ways to count. It had ended several romantic relationships and strained his relationship with his sister, who insisted the solitary goal of any language was to be understood. (Of course, she fancied herself an armchair linguist!)

The rules of grammar provided structure. Dictionaries should've been prescriptive, not descriptive. At this rate, any word, or variation of a word, could become "accepted" through mass misusage.

This was the hill on which he'd die.

twins

AT ONE POINT, they'd been identical twins. Now they were a before/after cautionary tale. One of the sisters had believed her breasts were too small, her nose was too big, her butt was too small, and her body needed artwork to appear not so ordinary. The other sister didn't seem to mind any of the things about her appearance that had bothered her twin and had spent more of her time living a life outside of anyone's gaze. Social media mattered to one but not the other. One was remarkably happy; the other chased something just outside her reach.

names

64

HER MOTHER HAD GIVEN her a name that was easy to pronounce but hard to spell. It was a beautiful name, but when she went to spell it for people, she could see them cringe. It wasn't even phonetic. Some of the letters were silent. To make matters worse, her mother called her by a nickname that was short, simple, and easy to spell. Why hadn't she been given *that* name instead? She pondered this when she went to meet with a lawyer about getting her name legally changed. In the end, though, she held on to her given name.

simpatico

THEY MET at a summer basement party in Atlanta, both introverts who thought of themselves as sitting "off to the side" to watch others dance to old school neo soul beneath the blue lights. As they sat next to each other, a conversation sparked like flint on steel, and their postures shifted to face each other. They talked through several albums worth of music, all the while inching closer and closer together. When the party ended and the lights came up, they reluctantly released their embrace.

They could have exchanged numbers, but they figured no moment could've top that one.

purple

THE OFFICIAL COLOR for their wedding was mauve, though they found themselves debating exactly what that color was. She thought the color leaned more toward magenta, so she selected dresses for her bridesmaids using a pinkish palette. He thought the color leaned more toward purple, so he selected ties that were boldly purple. In the end, their wedding included very little that was actually mauve, and many of the attendees complimented them on their use of purple and pink as wedding colors. It wasn't the last time their contradictory perspectives would yield a favorable result, though. Just ask their kids.

part four
writers

aira

SHE'D DISCOVERED the book in the back of an old bookstore, beneath a stack of neglected, used tomes. She'd never heard of the author before. Apparently the book had been the only of his oeuvre to be translated into English. It was a rather thin volume from a prolific Argentinian author whose writing style was said to have influenced a generation of South American writers.

She read the first few pages and caught a glimpse of the labyrinth that lay ahead. That book would later influence her, too, as she, having never written before, began to write her own stories.

baldwin

I AM NOT much to look at, I know. My teeth, my skin, my hair, my eyes are not what *you* would call beautiful, if you only appreciated the exterior, but my words—oh, my words—they are so beautiful as to be blinding, because my soul is beautiful, my being is beautiful, and that beauty refuses to remain cloaked in the ugly rags your mind would assign them. There is truth in my beauty, but neither my truth nor my beauty are readily accepted by all. Some would prefer to ignore my beauty, as it illuminates their own ugliness.

butler

Her typewriter is a crystal ball, revealing possibilities and probabilities, many of which trickle through into the realm of reality, a phoenix of sorts, where we find ourselves reborn within the ashes of our pasts, amidst the clacking of her keys, and transported beyond the sphere of our understanding. To be Black outside of what we have known as Blackness, to be represented in space, beyond time, within the hidden, infinite places of our awareness, she wills us, one story at a time, her arms wrapped around us, protecting us, assuring our progeny will have a place in the future.

borges

HE WANTED to be the kind of author they spoke about with effusive hyperbole, the kind whom, after he passed away, they spoke about in hushed tones of reverence, hoping to decipher what he might have thought about this or that, often straying from any semblance of a thought he would have actually possessed, because his presence lived outside of time, like a soul roaming an infinite library, a specter kissing the spines of books from which they continually built their ivory castles, and in the heart of that august cavern, they would dine on his words like ravenous wolves.

carver

Their MFA professor had a predilection for white male writers, blue collar storytellers who preferred the short story to the novel. He assigned several of one author's books, asking them to tackle similar themes in their own works. He even went so far as to offer a monetary prize to any student who could write a story that felt like it could've been written by that writer. The entries were submitted blindly, and a Black woman won the contest. Astonished she could mimic his idol, the professor never realized her true genius was in satirizing both him and the writer.

davis

ELLE EST PETITE, tout comme ses histoires.

But within them is something much bigger, something that expands in your mind, the cusp of an iceberg like a child standing on tippy-toe trying to see a swan in the distance.

The blueprint is her own, her words the antithesis of those whom she translates, those for whom she serves as a bridge for us to understand what greatness is, her own words fashioning a different bridge of brilliance, showing us how structurally sound the smallest story can be, the whispers of characters who reside in the quiet spaces of our minds.

due

HE LOVED HER, although she often scared him. A vacation was not complete unless they toured some haunted antebellum mansion or visited a place with a history so tragic the ghosts visited him in his dreams. Several times a month he went with her to see the latest horror movie, her arm wrapped tightly around his. When she jumped, he jumped even more. Then afterwards they would release their fears into the sweat-soaked sheets of their king-size bed. He longed to ask her about her fascination with these things, but he didn't. His love for her didn't require an explanation.

ellison

WHILE HE WAS at times lauded for his work, at no point in his career did he ever write a master-piece, something unanimously agreed upon by his peers to be worthy of the canon. He wondered if that was better for him, or if it would have been better to write a single work that checked all of the boxes. He'd read about writers struggling to live up to their classic works. He didn't have that problem, though at times he wished that he did, that he'd put it all into a single book and left the world wanting more.

faulkner

SHE WILL WALK the streets of Oxford draped in old money, holding on to an oak walking cane said to belong to her great-grandfather. She will prop herself up on this cane, both literally and figuratively.

The townspeople will see her slow amble from a distance, her body slumped beneath the weight of old money, and they will marvel at what she's become, feeling both pride and pity, a guilty nostalgia.

They will tell their children stories of when she was great, of the time when they, too, were great, though, deep down, they will be ashamed of their pride.

hemingway

He holds onto a red balloon. The balloon is bigger than his house. The balloon is his house.

He soars above trees. His laces hang toward earth. He breathes cold air.

The balloon shrinks a little. His sneakers touch leaves. He walks across canopies. He holds tight to his balloon.

The balloon is now smaller than his house. It is no longer his house.

He walks across branches. The balloon can no longer hold him.

He touches the earth again. His balloon withers beside him.

The balloon has become a large piece of rubber.

He will now mourn the balloon.

king

He paid for his movie ticket that opening weekend, excited to see the adaptation of his favorite novel into a big-budget blockbuster. As he sat there, mindlessly feeding himself popcorn, unable to look away from the screen, he wondered how his favorite scene from the novel would translate on screen.

Then the moment came. The protagonist was bound to a bed, on the cusp of being hobbled. And the antagonist emerged, her thick hands wrapped around the handle of—

A sledgehammer.

A sledgehammer?

Seriously?

Where was the axe? Where was the blowtorch?

Sure, the acting was good, but so what?

larson

SHE LOVED the simplicity of using a single panel. What could be more minimalist than that, more microfiction than that? She'd tried stories consisting of 100 words, 50 words, and even six words, but the single panel cartoon was the finest form of brevity, almost like the adage "a picture speaks a thousand words." She stared at each panel, laughing at cows and aliens and old ladies and silly men, forgetting for the moment she was looking at ink and paper. The one that cracked her up most was of a kid at a gifted school pushing a "pull" door.

morrison

THEY WATCHED as the large black bird flew across the sky and marveled at how majestic it appeared, despite the deep scars across its wings and the links clinking free of its talons. Larger than a bald eagle, its wingspan swathed patches of the earth in its shadow, even as it soared at dizzying altitudes. It was never supposed to leave the ground, though, and had been surrounded by turkeys and chickens and taught to wait for farmer feed: handouts of corn and soybeans. Now it dove down like lightning, selecting its own prey before returning to the endless sky.

murakami

SHE WAS a cat in sheep's clothing, her feline walk pushing him into the corner of a memory he thought he'd buried beneath the jazz chords of a his father's piano. She'd brought him into this labyrinthine library through purrs and bleats, this fugue, where little made sense other than the uncanny desire to pet her, touch her, tell her it was okay to not pretend she was something other than the love of his life, the mother of his children, but he knew she wouldn't stay, that she'd retreat into the sands of his hour glass like a dream.

naylor

She stands before an enormous brick wall, a chisel in one hand, a wooden mallet in the other. She will attack this wall with a vengeance. Everything that it represents—racism, classism, sexism, ageism, ablism, and the plethora of other "isms" that fester like infections awaiting a host—will crumble, piece by piece, onto a cracked pavement, slicked with blood and sweat. The reverberations of each strike will be felt from Brewster Place to Linden Hills, and there will be a silent acknowledgment and appreciation for the wall's death—but also an appreciation for the woman who brought it down.

petry

She elected to do her dissertation around the work of a bestselling writer from the Harlem Renaissance, one for whom there wasn't much scholarship, and for years she researched everything she could get her hands on. After successfully defending her dissertation, she learned the writer was still alive, living a quiet life away from the spotlight, so she decided to reach out to her to thank her for her contributions to the canon. Maybe it was simply bad timing, but the writer, markedly rude and dismissive, left her realizing that sometimes it was better to never meet your literary heroes.

roth

WHEN HE BECAME serious about writing, he read everything the Bard of Newark had written and immediately became fixated on the liberation of an author writing about masturbation. Maybe he would write about masturbation, too.

His literary agent disagreed with his choice.

"A white man can write about masturbation and it be okay. Black men aren't afforded the same freedom. There is an exoticism about darker penises, and the story would be lost beneath that quiet fascination."

He decided to write his masturbation story anyway, but he never attempted to publish it, fearing his literary agent may have been right.

styron

In Newport News, Virginia, there is a small residential/business community named after a fictitious city based off the city itself, the streets named after various famous authors, selected by a famous author, and there is a eponymously named square in this community, and along the street that runs across the face of this square is the name of the leader of a slave rebellion (who happens to have been the subject of one of said author's bestselling books), and along this street live the very people who would likely have been slain by this street's namesake many years ago.

walker

SHE HAS ONE "I" in her name, and I have none. Yet, we both found our ways to Atlanta in the beginning. Then New York. I have read her, though she probably has no idea of whom I am. We have the same surname. Maybe the masters of our ancestors were related. I imagine we write because we have to, because we see pieces of the Black American story yet untold in the growing canon. And then there's that thing about purple. Maybe one day we'll meet and have a conversation—about what?—I have no idea. Blackness? Our names?

wilson

I HAVE PERFECTED my cog in the machine. I know my job inside out. I even smell of the machine, taking it home in the evenings to my wife. She would not recognize me without its smell, without its grease smudged over me. She knows I work on the machine, one Black man on a never-ending assembly line of Black men, there to support the infrastructure of a machine, the entirety of which is completely unknown to me. But I must do my job to keep things running along. America will surely fall apart if I don't play my part.

part five
language

pronouns

IT HAD TAKEN them a while to use that particular pronoun in public, always fearing what others might think, but in that moment, they felt a freedom they had never experienced, and while the judgment of others may have rested just beyond the scope of their periphery, none of it mattered in that moment—and like that, the world changed, or at least their place within it, and the understanding of a person's need to be completely and totally authentic with not only themselves, but with the world around them, was one of the greatest gifts one could give themselves.

nouns

92

A MAN STOOD on the corner of Third and Main, holding a leather briefcase. Inside that briefcase was an idea, one he felt could change the world. There was nothing particularly special about the briefcase, but that did not prevent two kids on a moped from speeding by and depriving him of it anyway. He watched in anguish and surprise as the briefcase moved beyond his grasp.

He wondered what they would do when they opened it. Would they recognize the genius of the idea, or would they simply discard it?

He would always wonder what became of that idea.

verbs

HE COMES TO, running, always moving, through sickness and fatigue, his legs constantly pushing, his calves bulging with lactic acid, his shins tender, nearly numb to the fire that rages across them—but he is moving forward, because time stops for no one, and what else is life but putting one foot in front of the other? Toward what, though? Death? Infinity—or better yet the infinity of one's mind? It doesn't matter, though, because the destination is a matter of the direction he runs in, and he has been running so long he no longer remembers where he's going.

adverbs

Slowly. Carefully. Deliberately. These were the words he chanted silently to himself, as he looked at the wires. He'd seen this done in plenty of movies where the stakes were so high he could hardly stand it, and always, at the last second, the protagonist pulled the correct wire, preventing an enormous detonation.

But this wasn't a movie, and there was no word to describe how alert he felt in this moment.

Slowly. Carefully. Deliberately. This was the mantra *he* created, not one given to him by his instructors at the academy.

He would do his job. Slowly. Carefully. Deliberately.

adjectives

THE WORDS WERE HYPERBOLIC, effusive, but necessary (as far as he was concerned), his prose so purple it could have been easily amputated, but she demanded the fullness of his vocabulary, of his awareness, of his attention. He was not above creating new words, whether portmanteaux or neologisms, as long as they flowed from his mouth like ethereal melodies that would shower her perfection in its appropriate, complementary glow.

It would have been far simpler to tell her that he loved her, but some feelings seemed to expand beyond those elementary words and seek to break free of all language.

prepositions

96

His grandfather loved listening to the blues, the kind that still got played in juke joints out in the wet part of the county. He would sing along, emphasizing the words like a preacher.

"You know what it mean when she say he gotta stand up in it?" his grandfather asked.

"I have a pretty good idea," he responded.

"She say you can lick it and stroke it, but you ain't done shit if you can't stand up in it."

He could only nod. His grandfather was imparting generational wisdom, and he'd absorb as much of it as he could.

conjunctions

97

AND SO, as fate would have it, he couldn't find the key to open the final door of the labyrinth. He'd travelled miles along the meandering path, and he had periodically checked his pocket so this very thing would not happen. But here he was, despite all of his studied precautions, standing outside the door, too far from the entrance of the maze, with only the ultimate prize in front of him.

He tried fashioning a twig into the shape of the key, a rudimentary attempt at best, but he failed. The key was somewhere out there, just not here.

interjections

The pivotal "oh shit!" happened when he realized he wasn't as good a poet as he'd thought, so he became a critic—often demeaning those he viewed as more talented than he. Hoping to become great through death, he took arsenic. As he lay dying, he penned what he considered to be his finest work and left it on his nightstand.

At his wake, many of the poets he'd eviscerated in life came to pay their respects, but all they could talk about was how cliché his final poem turned out to be.

idioms

"WHAT's up with that fight you had last Friday?" she asked.

"I took him all the way down," he responded, locking an imaginary head in the muscular crook of his arm. "A piece of cake, I tell you."

"I wish I could step up and take the plunge." She sighed.

"There's nothing to it but to do it."

"I keep wondering if someone will get the better of me."

He nodded. " I feel you, but you can't live life in fear of the next man."

"Easy for you to say."

"Nah. You just have to tap into your inner dog."

similes

Notorious like Christopher Wallace, like Chris and Em's dead wrong, like Shakespeare's notorious wrong, like Duran Duran's no-no-notorious, like people who like using infamous and famous interchangeably, like Tommy guns and gangsters you only convict with tax fraud, like Kim missing Chris, like Wilshire and South Fairfax or the Strip or a Queens studio, like chewed ears in boxing rings, like an all-white jury in Mississippi in 1955, like Skittles and Arizona tea, like failed Aryan art students, like queens and cakes or queens and horses, like sneaker messiahs, like reality show politicians, like thousands of similes, like simply notorious.

motif

He has finally gotten used to falling through the holes. They appear everywhere: at the foot of his bed, just outside his front door, on the sidewalk by the bus stop, in the food court at the mall. These holes randomly appear, his feet ambling along then—*poof*—it's there, and without warning, he drops down what feels like a hundred feet and falls into his bed at home. He never knows when they will occur, but he has accepted that this is now a part of his daily routine and that whatever he does, he must always be ready.

foreshadowing

She had revealed to him that she was emotionally unavailable, that she needed time to recover from her previous relationship, which took various tolls on her spirit, and he had heard all of that, but then they went out and spent several amazing evenings together, each of these capped by intimate moments that restored his faith in relationships, so he continued to woo her, and she allowed herself to be wooed, and he fell hard for her and allowed the word to escape his lips, but she politely reminded him of her earlier warning and wished him well without her.

irony

THE GIFT WAS DESIGNED to be a prank. She'd purchased the stuffed monkey's paw online. She figured since he was a fan of both the short story and the movie director (whose production company shared the same name), he would get a kick out of it.

"What are your three wishes?" she asked jokingly.

"I'm sorry," he responded.

"What do you mean?"

"I've already made my wishes."

"What are they?" she asked.

"I can't tell you."

"Do they impact me?" She was now growing more concerned.

He didn't respond and tucked the monkey's paw in his pocket.

"Sorry," he said.

plot

There is much ado about what constitutes a story. Dogmatic philosophies fill the academies, and a scholar is likely to look at this story as something other than a story (a micro essay, maybe?) because Aristotle said every story should have a beginning, middle, and end; Freytag was convinced of the need for exposition, rising action, climax, falling action, and a denouement; and the hero's journey was a series of trials and tribulations resulting in the evolution of the protagonist. So this is not a story, even though there's a beginning, middle, and end, and the author, too, has evolved?

pov

You look at me a bit longer than would make me feel comfortable, and I feel compelled to tell you the truth, the thing I've been hiding from you, that this no longer works for me, that I have goals I want to accomplish in life that I can't do with you here, demanding my time and energy, at times making me feel too small for my dreams, inadequate, reliant on you. There is no question right now, except the one in your eyes, and I feel my lips part. I will tell you the truth—eventually—just not today.

genre

SHE REALIZED, only after she published her tenth book, that she'd been writing the same story over and over. The protagonists were all the same, all had the same motivations, and the stories pretty much wrote themselves. When she'd first begun to write, she'd imagined she would write across genres, telling stories that mirrored those of her favorite authors, but instead of exploring these disparate ideas, she found herself writing about the same three relationships she'd experienced in college.

She wondered if her readers knew she had only one story to tell, that she was incapable of writing anything else.

symbolism

She resides in a house on a block in the back of her mind, blocks propping it up so that it is elevated above the sweeping, rushing waters. Try as she might, she can't block the sound of the waves below. Her laptop rests on blocks, and next to it is a cup filled with blocks of ice that couldn't dissolve in acid. Her TV is a skinny block of plastic stuck to a wall, its signal blocked by some unknown source. But from the block of paper on her desk, she plans to write her book when she's unblocked.

prologue

She knew there was a story before the story (there was always a story before the story), but the editors told her she shouldn't tell it, that she should learn to tell her story without that part. So she did. And the story was good—well, as good as it could be—and people bought lots of copies of it and enjoyed it thoroughly, assuring there would be sequels. Still, she knew the story was incomplete. She often wondered about the prologue that she'd cut from her book and whether it would have really made a difference in the end.

epigraph

His poetry was disjointed and unorganized, in need of an editor (or two), but people recognized his talent, his gift of rhythm, of language, of imagery. The whole of it, though, was, at best, inconsistent. Needing some elaborate explanation for this quirk, critics labeled this a "style" of poetry, thereby creating an invitation for other poets to explore these techniques in their own works. And so there is a generation of disjointed and unorganized poets thinking themselves geniuses—and a group of fiction writers who have learned their poetry is best when stripped to its essence and used for epigraphs.

acknowledgments

SHE BOUGHT his book on publication day, even though she'd told herself that she wouldn't. She'd watched him sit there and stare at a blank screen for hours. She'd witnessed all of the false starts. She'd even bought a bottle of cheap wine from the corner store to toast the completion of the first draft. This was before the bidding war. This was before the money. This was before the whispers of awards to come. This was before he decided he no longer needed her. Still, she bought the book, hoping that he'd at least mentioned her in the acknowledgments.

acknowledgments

Thank you to my beautiful wife, Lauren, and my amazing daughter, Zoë.

Additional thanks to my brother, Torrey, and his family; my parents, Jean and Randolph; the Walker, Holbrook, Maxie, Whittley, and Williams families; the Dumas Collective; my colleagues at Hampton University; the staff of *Writer's Digest* magazine; the James River Writers; my Zeta Phi Beta Sigma family; and my team at WorldSpark Studios.

about the author

Ran Walker (he/him) is the author of 31 books. His short stories, flash fiction, microfiction, and poetry have appeared in a variety of anthologies and journals. Prior to becoming a writer and educator, he worked in magazine publishing and practiced law in Mississippi.

He is the winner of the Indie Author Project's 2019 National Indie Author of the Year Award (selected by judges from *Library Journal, Publishers Weekly*, IngramSpark, St. Martin's Press, and *Writer's Digest*), the 2019 Black Caucus of the American Library Association Best Fiction Ebook Award, the 2018 Virginia Indie Author Project Award for Adult Fiction, and the 2021 Blind Corner Afrofuturism Microfiction Contest. Ran is an Associate Professor of English and Creative Writing at Hampton University and serves as a Contributing Editor with *Writer's Digest*. He lives in Virginia with his wife and much better half, Lauren, and his amazing daughter, Zoë.

also by ran walker

B-Sides and Remixes

30 Love: A Novel

Mojo's Guitar: A Novel/(Il était une fois Morris Jones)

Afro Nerd in Love: A Novella

The Keys of My Soul: A Novel

The Race of Races: A Novel

The Illest: A Novella

Bessie, Bop, or Bach: Collected Stories

Four Floors (with Sabin Prentis)

Black Hand Side: Stories

White Pages: A Novel

She Lives in My Lap

Reverb

Work-In-Progress

Daykeeper

Most of My Heroes Don't Appear On No Stamps

Portable Black Magic: Tales of the Afro Strange

The Strange Museum: 50-Word Stories

Bees + Things + Flowers: Microfictions

The World Is Yours: Microfictions

Can I Kick It?: Sneaker Microfiction and Poetry

The Golden Book: A 50-Year Marriage Told In 50-Word Stories

Keep It 100: 100-Word Stories

A Burst of Gray: A Novel In 100-Word Stories

The Library of Afro Curiosities: 100-Word Stories

Black Marker: A Novel in 100-Word Stories

GloKat and the Art of Timing: A Novel in 100-Word Stories

A Different Kind of Christmas Story: A Carol in 100-Word Stories

Spaceships Don't Come Equipped with Rearview Mirrors: 50-Word Stories

This Is Not a Poem/Story: 100-Word Stories

www.ingramcontent.com/pod-product-compliance
Lightning Source LLC
Chambersburg PA
CBHW040229170726
48295CB00014B/857